For Andrea and Leonie

For more information about our books, and the authors and artists
who create them, visit our web site: www.northsouth.com

A Michael Neugebauer Book

Hubert and the Apple Tree

By Bruno Hächler
Illustrated by Albrecht Rissler
Translated by Rosemary Lanning

NORTH-SOUTH BOOKS · New York/London

Hubert lived at the edge of a small
town. He was a friendly man with
a mop of curly brown hair, small
round spectacles, and kindly twin-
kling eyes. His wooden house had
grown crooked with age.
It stood far back from the street,
coyly concealing itself behind
a large, spreading apple tree in
a meadow strewn with wild flowers.
Every morning, when Hubert
looked out at that beautiful tree,
his spirits rose.
Every evening, when he came home
from work, he would sit by his
window and watch the birds in the
tree's leafy crown.

There is more to watching trees than you might think, because they are constantly changing. In spring, they deck themselves in dazzling blossom while their new leaves unfurl in the warm sunshine, and bees buzz around them, looking for nectar. In summer, when the hot sun blazes down, people are grateful for the cool, green shade they offer. In autumn, the wind toys with their tawny leaves, and scatters them carelessly across the fields and streets. Then winter comes and blankets their bare branches with snow.

Hubert often lay under his apple tree, remembering how he had climbed it as a child. All too often he had hidden in its thick canopy of leaves when his mother called him to come indoors before he was ready.

Whenever he looked at his tree,
Hubert was indescribably happy.
He felt he had all he could possibly
want from life.
Sometimes people stopped outside
his fence and exclaimed,
"Look at that tree! Isn't it lovely!"
But most of them hurried past,
too preoccupied to stop.

Years went by. Hubert was growing older. Deep furrows etched his face. His hair turned white, thinned, and fell like autumn leaves. His beard grew longer and thicker. Hubert was still a happy man, and he still spent hours watching his tree and the birds.

Sometimes he caught mischievous children stealing his apples, but he never scolded them. "Forbidden fruit always tastes better, doesn't it?" he said with a chuckle.

Then, one autumn day, something terrible happened. Stormy winds were rattling the shutters and fallen leaves whirled high in the air. Billowing storm clouds rolled over the nearby hills, turning the sky so black that people took fright and ran indoors. At the first rumble of thunder, Hubert closed his windows and watched the approaching storm from behind the glass. Raindrops clattered against the window panes. Then a heavy shower poured down like a waterfall on the small town. Lightning flared and crackled, and the thunder-claps grew louder and more menacing. Suddenly, Hubert's heart stood still. He saw a huge bolt of lightning strike his apple tree. There was a deafening crash. The tree groaned, and its trunk split open. Cooling rain ran into the wound.

The storm had passed. Hubert
hurried out to his apple tree.
How sad it looked now — as gnarled
and crooked as the old house.
Its trunk was split right down to its
sturdy roots.
"That must hurt," Hubert whispered,
tenderly stroking the tree. It seemed
to sigh. To Hubert, the gleaming
drops of water on its bark looked
like tears.

The following spring was warm and
sunny. Birds sang. Flowers bloomed.
The only sad sight was the gnarled
old apple tree.
A few tiny leaves had sprouted here
and there, and bees buzzed around
its scattered blossoms but, try as
it might, the old apple tree could
never regain its former glory.

Its scar still ached when the weather turned suddenly cold, or especially hot. But something even worse was happening: people now stopped and stared at it.
"Look at that ugly thing!" they said.
"What an eyesore!"

"Someone ought to cut it down,"
a woman said. The man with her
agreed.
"They could park a few cars here,
or make a proper lawn if they
cleared that old tree away."
Hubert was angry. He loved his tree
just as it was. Every evening he
went and stroked its bark. If he saw
people staring he shouted,
"Go away!" and ran at them,
brandishing a broom. But it was no
use. The next day there would be
more of them, staring and muttering.
Then Hubert had an idea.

Hubert rode off on his rusty bicycle, smiling mysteriously. When he came back a few hours later, he was carrying a big bundle. He fetched a spade and began to dig next to the old tree. He didn't stop until he had dug a deep, round hole. Then he planted a sapling in it: a sturdy young apple tree, scarcely tall enough to reach the end of his snow-white beard.

At last he's getting rid of that ugly old tree, people thought. But Hubert still smiled his mysterious smile. He covered the little tree's roots with soil, watered it well and put the spade away.

Years passed. Seasons came and
went. Hubert, an old man now, spent
many hours sitting contentedly by
his window. The sapling had grown
into a splendid apple tree, laden
with more fruit than Hubert could
ever eat. The old, gnarled tree
still stood in the shelter of the
younger one.

Happy and at peace, the old tree
took pride in the few leaves and
blossoms it bravely bore each
spring. If a child stole its fruit,
it secretly smiled.

People now hurried by once again
without a glance at the two trees.
Few stopped to enjoy the sight of
them.

One autumn evening, the tree felt
a familiar hand on its furrowed bark.
Old Hubert whispered something,
and the tree nodded. They had both
sensed it. Winter was coming.
There was snow in the air. It was
time to rest.

Hubert took to his bed and, as
snowflakes danced outside the
window, the old tree lay down too.
And they both slept peacefully,
dreaming of spring.